...sody sallyraytus, lickety-split...

Beware, Beware of the Big Bad Bear!

Beware, Beware of the Big Bad Bear!

By Dianne de Las Casas   Illustrated by Marita Gentry

PELICAN PUBLISHING COMPANY
Gretna 2012

To my "sody-lightful" Tennessee gals—Beth Jackson, Allison Roberts, Nancy Dickinson, Diane Chen, and LeAnna Dendy. I <3 U!

To my sister, Missy, and my brothers, Eric and Charles—fun family is a "bear" necessity of life!

The word "Pelican" and the depiction of a pelican are trademarks of Pelican Publishing Company, Inc., and are registered in the U.S. Patent and Trademark Office.

Library of Congress Cataloging-in-Publication Data

de Las Casas, Dianne.
  Beware, beware of the big bad bear! / by Dianne de Las Casas ; illustrated by Marita Gentry.
    p. cm.
  Summary: When one after another family member goes to the store for baking soda and never returns, the pet squirrel decides to investigate in this retelling of a traditional Appalachian tale. Includes a recipe for soda biscuits.
  ISBN 978-1-4556-1690-9 (hardcover : alk. paper) -- ISBN 978-1-4556-1691-6 (e-book) [1. Folklore--Appalachian Region.] I. Gentry, Marita, ill. II. Title.
  PZ8.1.D367Bew 2012
  398.20974'045--dc23
  [E]
                        2011052875

Printed in Singapore

Published by Pelican Publishing Company, Inc.
1000 Burmaster Street, Gretna, Louisiana 70053

BEWARE, BEWARE OF THE BIG BAD BEAR!

Once there lived Paw Paw, Maw Maw, Beau, Belle, and their pet, Squirrel. One day, Maw Maw wanted to bake beautiful, buttery biscuits, but she was out of sody sallyraytus.

So she told Beau to go to the store, but before he went, Maw
Maw said, "Beware, beware of the big bad bear!"
When Beau got to the store, he said,

"I need sody sallyraytus, lickety-split.
Maw Maw's going to bake some biscuits with it."

After he bought the sody, Beau started to cross the bridge, but underneath lived the

big bad bear.

The bear said, "I'm going to eat you up—you and your sody sallyraytus." He opened his big bear mouth and gobbled Beau up, just like that.

When Beau did not come home, Maw Maw said, "That boy is taking too long!" So Maw Maw sent Belle to the store, but before she went, Maw Maw said, "Beware, beware of the big bad bear!"
When Belle got to the store, she said,

*"I need sody sallyraytus, lickety-split.
Maw Maw's going to bake some biscuits with it."*

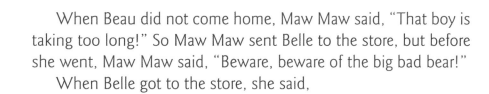

After she bought the sody, Belle started to cross the bridge, but underneath lived the

big bad bear.

The bear said, "I ate the little boy and now I'm going to eat you up—you and your sody sallyraytus." He opened his big bear mouth and gobbled Belle up, just like that.

When Belle did not come home, Maw Maw said, "That girl is taking too long!" So Maw Maw sent Paw Paw to the store, but before he went, Maw Maw said, "Beware, beware of the big bad bear!"

When Paw Paw got to the store, he said,

"I need sody sallyraytus, lickety-split.
Maw Maw's going to bake some biscuits with it."

After he bought the sody, Paw Paw started
to cross the bridge, but underneath lived the

big bad bear.

The bear said, "I ate the little boy, I ate the little girl, and now I'm going to eat you up—you and your sody sallyraytus." He opened his big bear mouth and gobbled Paw Paw up, just like that.

When Paw Paw did not come home, Maw Maw said, "That old man is taking too long! I'll fetch it myself." So Maw Maw went to the store, but before she went, Squirrel said, "Beware, beware of the big bad bear!"

When Maw Maw got to the store, she said,

"I need sody sallyraytus, lickety-split.
I'm a-going to bake some biscuits with it."

After she bought her sody, Maw Maw started
to cross the bridge, but underneath lived the

big bad bear.

The bear said, "I ate the little boy, I ate the
little girl, I ate the old man, and now
I'm going to eat you up—you and
your sody sallyraytus."

He opened his big bear mouth and gobbled Maw Maw up, just like that.

Now Squirrel was by herself, getting hungrier and hungrier.
She said, "I'll fetch it myself." So Squirrel went to the store.
When Squirrel got to the store, she said,

"I need sody sallyraytus, lickety-split.
I'm a-going to bake some biscuits with it."

After she bought her sody, Squirrel started to cross the bridge, but underneath lived the

big bad bear.

The bear said, "I ate the little boy, I ate the little girl, I ate the old man, I ate the old woman, and now I'm going to eat you up—you and your sody sallyraytus!"

Squirrel shook her tail, threw her sody sallyraytus at the bear, and said, "Oh no you won't!" Lickety-split, she scampered up a nearby tree. The big bad bear followed and began climbing the tree too.

Squirrel scampered to the end of a branch and teased, "Na-na-na-na-na-na!"

The bear growled, "If you can do it with your little legs, then I can do it with my big legs!"

But the small branch could not hold the
big bad bear, and it broke.

Squirrel jumped to another branch, and the big bad bear fell . . .

Dooooowwwnnn

UD!

The bear landed so hard that out bounced Beau, Belle, Maw Maw, and Paw Paw. And out bounced four boxes of sody sallyraytus! They had enough sody to bake a big batch of beautiful, buttery biscuits.

They sang a song on the way home.

*"We got sody sallyraytus, lickety-split.
Maw Maw's going to bake some biscuits with it."*

When they got home, sure enough, Maw Maw baked a big batch of beautiful, buttery biscuits. The family opened their big hungry mouths and gobbled the biscuits up . . .

JUST LIKE THAT!

Sody Sallyraytus

MAW MAW'S SIMPLE SODY BISCUITS

2 cups flour
3/4 tsp. baking soda
1 tsp. sugar
1/2 tsp. salt
1 stick (1/2 cup) cold butter
1/4 cup apple cider vinegar
1/2 cup milk

In medium bowl, combine flour, baking soda, sugar, and salt. Cut in butter. Add vinegar and milk. Stir until dough is sticky. Using tablespoon, drop heaping spoonfuls onto greased cookie sheet. Bake at 450 degrees for 12-15 minutes or until golden brown. Makes 10-12 biscuits.

AUTHOR'S NOTE

Beware, Beware of the Big Bad Bear! is an adaptation of the Appalachian folktale "Sody Sallyraytus" (pronounced soh-dee sall-eeh-ray-tuss), which means baking soda. In the South, we love buttery biscuits. Maw Maw's biscuits are the "drop" kind, which are easiest for kids to make. Gobble them up . . .

JUST LIKE THAT!

...sody sallyraytus, lickety-split...